MR. RUDE

Roger Hargreaves

Written and illustrated by
Adam Hargreaves

Mr Rude is rude.

He is very rude.

He is very, very rude.

He is worse than very, very rude.

He is extraordinarily rude.

When you meet somebody, you might think to yourself that that person has a large nose, but you wouldn't say anything to them, would you?

Because that would be rude, wouldn't it?

Well, Mr Rude would just blurt it out.

"Big nose!"

But he wouldn't stop there.

Oh no, not Mr Rude.

"Big nose! With a nose like that you could vacuum the floor!"

Can you imagine saying that to someone?

Well, I hope you can't!

And he was the same with everyone.

If he met someone overweight he would shout, "Fatty! You're supposed to take the food out of the fridge, not eat the fridge as well!"

When he was driving along in his car he would yell rude things at the people he passed by.

Mr Rude was a horrible man who didn't have a nice thing to say to anyone and, not surprisingly, no-one liked him.

One day Mr Rude met Little Miss Tiny. (Or not so much met as nearly trod on her.)

"Good morning," said Little Miss Tiny.

"Look at the size of you!" exclaimed Mr Rude. "Squirt! You're so tiny I could squash you under my thumb!"

Poor Little Miss Tiny burst into tears and ran home.

Behind a tree on the other side of the lane Mr Happy looked anything but happy.

He had heard everything.

The next morning Mr Happy was outside Mr Rude's house, suitcase in hand.

Mr Happy knocked on Mr Rude's front door.

"Go away!" shouted Mr Rude.

Mr Happy knocked again.

Mr Rude opened the door.

"Can't you read," said Mr Rude, pointing to his doormat.

Mr Rude's doormat did not say 'welcome' like everyone else's doormat. Mr Rude had crossed out 'WELCOME' and then, in large black letters, had written 'GO AWAY!' underneath.

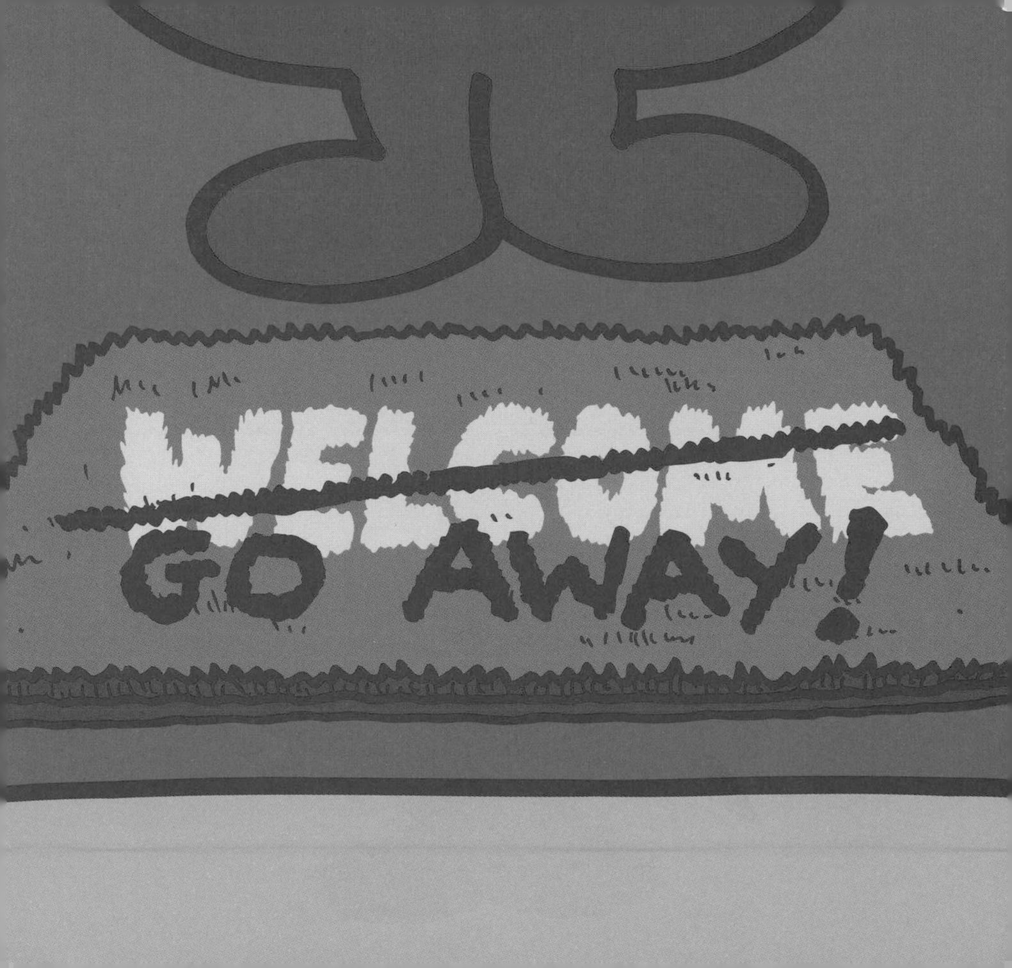
WELCOME
GO AWAY!

Mr Happy smiled, barged past Mr Rude and went into the living room.

"GET OUT!" shouted Mr Rude.

Mr Happy smiled an even larger smile and sat down in the armchair.

Mr Rude exploded. He ranted and raged for half an hour, but Mr Happy calmly sat through it all, smiling.

Eventually, Mr Rude went into the kitchen to make himself supper, without offering any to Mr Happy.

After his supper Mr Rude ranted and raged for a full hour, but, whatever Mr Rude called him, Mr Happy took no notice.

Finally, Mr Rude turned out the lights and went upstairs without offering Mr Happy a bed for the night.

When he came down in the morning Mr Happy was still there, still smiling.

"OK, I give in!" cried Mr Rude. "What do you want?"

"Breakfast would be nice," said Mr Happy. "Please."

Mr Rude made breakfast for him.

It was the first time in Mr Rude's life that he had ever done anything for someone else.

In fact, it was the first time he had ever asked anybody what they wanted.

"Thank you," said Mr Happy, when he had finished.

"Right! You can go now!" demanded Mr Rude.

But Mr Happy did not budge.

Mr Rude ranted and raged and raged and ranted, but he ended up making lunch for Mr Happy . . . and supper.

He even offered Mr Happy a bed that night.

Mr Happy stayed for a fortnight.

Slowly the ranting and raging became less and less.

Mr Rude discovered he had something that he had never known he possessed.

Manners!

When it was time for Mr Happy to leave he shook Mr Rude's hand and said, "Thank you so much, Mr Rude. I really enjoyed my stay."

Mr Rude beamed a smile that was every bit as wide as Mr Happy's and found himself saying, "And so did I."

Mr Rude was a changed man.

"Burp!" belched Mr Rude.

Well, almost!